Grandma's
Seaside
Bloomers

First published in 2007 by
Franklin Watts
338 Euston Road
London
NW1 3BH

Franklin Watts Australia
Level 17/207 Kent Street
Sydney
NSW 2000

A CIP catalogue record for this book is available
from the British Library.

ISBN 978 0 7496 7081 8 (hbk)
ISBN 978 0 7496 7412 0 (pbk)

Series Editor: Melanie Palmer
Series Advisor: Dr Barrie Wade
Series Designer: Peter Scoulding

Printed in China

Franklin Watts is a division of
Hachette Children's Books.

A Victorian seaside story for Marilyn – J.J.

HOPSCOTCH HISTORIES

Grandma's Seaside Bloomers

by Julia Jarman and Roger Fereday

W

FRANKLIN WATTS
LONDON•SYDNEY

About this book

In 1871 a new law made the first Monday in August a bank holiday. It was called a bank holiday because all banks were closed for the day, but it meant that no one had to work. Going to the seaside was a popular Victorian pastime on bank holidays. Places such as Brighton or Blackpool became regular holiday resorts, as they were easy to get to by train. The first Monday in August is still a bank holiday in Scotland and the Republic of Ireland. In 1971 in England, Wales and Northern Ireland, this holiday was changed to the last Monday in August.

Father was at home –

on a Monday!

"Why isn't Father at work today?"
asked Albert and Dora.
"Why are we in our best clothes?"
asked little Edward.

"Today's a bank holiday – nobody has to work!" said Father.
"Yes," said Grandma. "But we must still be properly dressed."

Then a horse and carriage arrived.

"Ooh, where are we going?"

asked Dora.

"Wait and see," said Grandma.

"Put on your hat, Dora. You

must be properly dressed."

"But I'm too hot," said Dora.

9

No one would tell them where they were going, but the carriage took them to Victoria train station.

Dora and Albert looked for clues.

"Are we going to ... ?"

"Children should be seen and
not heard!" said Grandma.

Everyone felt hot on the train.

"Neck tie, Albert. Hat, Edward!

Pull down your skirt, Dora!"

Grandma went on and on.

12

"We must all be properly dressed,"
she said again. Albert whispered:
"We must all be properly dressed."
Dora nearly laughed out loud.

At last they reached the seaside.
There was so much to see and do.
What would they do first?

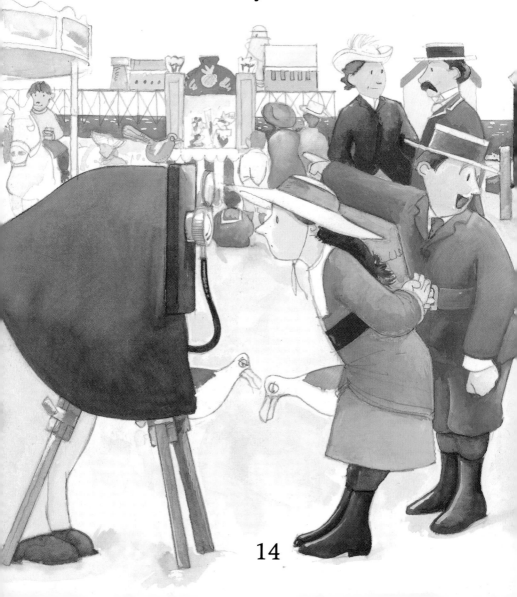

"Donkey rides!" cried Edward.

"The funfair!" said Albert.

"Silence!" said Grandma.

First, everyone watched a juggler.

Then they stopped to look through a telescope.

16

Grandma looked hot and cross.
People were not properly dressed –
and they were eating outside!

"I'm hungry," said Edward.

So Father took them for lunch

at the Grand Hotel.

Afterwards they went to the beach
and saw people bathing in the sea.
"Don't look!" cried Grandma.

But Mother said: "Let's go sea-bathing. It will cool us down."
"Yes," said Father. "Come on, we can use the bathing huts."

"You could take off your hat, Grandma," laughed Mother. "Never!" Grandma replied, though her face was as red as a tomato.

Horses pulled the bathing huts into the sea. Everyone jumped in.

"Splash you!" cried Albert.

"Splash you!" cried Dora.

Sea-bathing was exciting!

But when everyone got back to the beach there was no sign of Grandma. What had happened to her?

24

Had she melted in the heat?

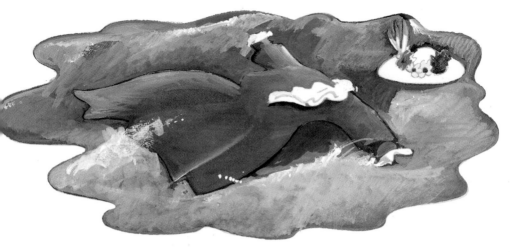

Had a big wave swept her away?

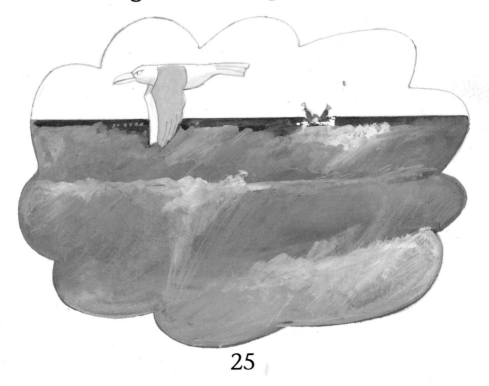

Soon everyone was looking for a
large lady in black. Father said:
"We must get a policeman to help."

But Albert and Dora had a better
idea. They raced to the promenade.

Dora could not see Grandma
anywhere. Then she saw a puffy
white cloud and started to laugh.

"That's not a cloud.
Look Albert! It's Grandma's
puffy white bloomers!"

Just then a gust of wind lifted

Grandma's skirt even higher!

"Grandma!" cried Dora.

"Please pull down your skirt."

"Grandmas should be heard and not seen," said Albert. And even Grandma laughed.

Hopscotch has been specially designed to fit the requirements of the National Literacy Strategy. It offers real books by top authors and illustrators for children developing their reading skills. There are 49 Hopscotch stories to choose from!

Marvin, the Blue Pig
ISBN 978 0 7496 4619 6

Plip and Plop
ISBN 978 0 7496 4620 2

The Queen's Dragon
ISBN 978 0 7496 4618 9

Flora McQuack
ISBN 978 0 7496 4621 9

Willie the Whale
ISBN 978 0 7496 4623 3

Naughty Nancy
ISBN 978 0 7496 4622 6

Run!
ISBN 978 0 7496 4705 6

The Playground Snake
ISBN 978 0 7496 4706 3

"Sausages!"
ISBN 978 0 7496 4707 0

The Truth about Hansel and Gretel
ISBN 978 0 7496 4708 7

Pippin's Big Jump
ISBN 978 0 7496 4710 0

Whose Birthday Is It?
ISBN 978 0 7496 4709 4

The Princess and the Frog
ISBN 978 0 7496 5129 9

Flynn Flies High
ISBN 978 0 7496 5130 5

Clever Cat
ISBN 978 0 7496 5131 2

Moo!
ISBN 978 0 7496 5332 3

Izzie's Idea
ISBN 978 0 7496 5334 7

Roly-poly Rice Ball
ISBN 978 0 7496 5333 0

I Can't Stand It!
ISBN 978 0 7496 5765 9

Cockerel's Big Egg
ISBN 978 0 7496 5767 3

How to Teach a Dragon Manners
ISBN 978 0 7496 5873 1

The Truth about those Billy Goats
ISBN 978 0 7496 5766 6

Marlowe's Mum and the Tree House
ISBN 978 0 7496 5874 8

Bear in Town
ISBN 978 0 7496 5875 5

The Best Den Ever
ISBN 978 0 7496 5876 2

ADVENTURE STORIES

Aladdin and the Lamp
ISBN 978 0 7496 6692 7

Blackbeard the Pirate
ISBN 978 0 7496 6690 3

George and the Dragon
ISBN 978 0 7496 6691 0

Jack the Giant-Killer
ISBN 978 0 7496 6693 4

TALES OF KING ARTHUR

1. The Sword in the Stone
ISBN 978 0 7496 6694 1

2. Arthur the King
ISBN 978 0 7496 6695 8

3. The Round Table
ISBN 978 0 7496 6697 2

4. Sir Lancelot and the Ice Castle
ISBN 978 0 7496 6698 9

TALES OF ROBIN HOOD

Robin and the Knight
ISBN 978 0 7496 6699 6

Robin and the Monk
ISBN 978 0 7496 6700 9

Robin and the Friar
ISBN 978 0 7496 6702 3

Robin and the Silver Arrow
ISBN 978 0 7496 6703 0

FAIRY TALES

The Emperor's New Clothes
ISBN 978 0 7496 7077 1 *
ISBN 978 0 7496 7421 2

Cinderella
ISBN 978 0 7496 7073 3 *
ISBN 978 0 7496 7417 5

Snow White
ISBN 978 0 7496 7074 0 *
ISBN 978 0 7496 7418 2

Jack and the Beanstalk
ISBN 978 0 7496 7078 8 *
ISBN 978 0 7496 7422 9

The Three Billy Goats Gruff
ISBN 978 0 7496 7076 4 *
ISBN 978 0 7496 7420 5

The Pied Piper of Hamelin
ISBN 978 0 7496 7075 7 *
ISBN 978 0 7496 7419 9

HISTORIES

Toby and the Great Fire of London
ISBN 978 0 7496 7079 5 *
ISBN 978 0 7496 7410 6

Pocahontas the Peacemaker
ISBN 978 0 7496 7080 1 *
ISBN 978 0 7496 7411 3

Grandma's Seaside Bloomers
ISBN 978 0 7496 7081 8 *
ISBN 978 0 7496 7412 0

Hoorah for Mary Seacole
ISBN 978 0 7496 7082 5 *
ISBN 978 0 7496 7413 7

Remember the 5th of November
ISBN 978 0 7496 7083 2 *
ISBN 978 0 7496 7414 4

Tutankhamun and the Golden Chariot
ISBN 978 0 7496 7084 9 *
ISBN 978 0 7496 7415 1

* hardback